Hello,

Oh, please don't look inside the pages of this **book**.

Turn around and
quickly **run** ...

THIS BOOK
BELONGS TO

SCHOOL of MONSTERS

By Sally Rippin

BRUNO WON'T DANCE

Art by Chris Kennett

Kane Miller
A DIVISION OF EDC PUBLISHING

Monsters dance outside one **day**.

SPIN

Bruno stares
from far **away**.

TAP TAP
TAP

3

"Why don't you dance?"
says Teacher **Pat**.

Bruno says,
"I can't do **that!**

"Wolves don't dance.
They growl and **run!**"

RAH   GROWL

Teacher smiles.
"But dancing's **fun!**"

Pat thinks hard of what to **do**

BEEP
BEEP
BOOP

DAN

to help dear Bruno
join in, **too**.

The next day when it's time to **play**

the monsters hear their teacher **say**:

"Today we're going to the **hall.**

There's someone here
to meet you **all**."

They cheer as loudly as they **can**

when through the door ...

... walks Wolfman Dan!

Dan busts a move,
spins on his **head**.

JUMP

FLIP

WHIZZ

The monsters roar,
their faces **red**.

"Wow, he's the best!"
the monsters **say**.

"Stay cool!" says Dan,
then glides **away**.

"Did you know wolves could dance like **that**?"

Bruno shrugs and smiles at **Pat**.

"I did!" says Pat.
"You should feel **proud**.

NUDGE
NUDGE

Let's play some music, extra **loud**.”

"Show us, Bruno!
That's so **cool**!"

"Hey, we could start our own dance **school**!"

The monsters dance out in the **sun**.

Pat watches Bruno having **fun.**

"You'll be a dancer,
just like **Dan!**"

The others yell,
"Oh yes, you **can!**"

But Bruno grins and
turns to **say,**

"I'd rather teach like YOU one **day**!"

NEW WORDS TO LEARN

Find words with the letter **a** in them. How does **a** sound different in each word?

START HERE

NEXT LEVEL

WELL DONE

day

that

fun

Dan

do

head

proud

run

hall

Pat

play

can

too

away

red

school

say

all

sun

loud

cool

HOW TO USE THIS BOOK

for adults reading with children

Welcome to the School of Monsters!

Here are some tips for helping your child learn to read.

At first, your child will be happy just to listen to you read aloud. Reading to your child is a great way for them to associate books with enjoyment and love, as well as to become familiar with language. Talk to them about what is going on in the pictures and ask them questions about what they see. As you read aloud, follow the words with your finger from left to right.

Once your child has started to receive some basic reading instruction, you might like to point out the words in **bold**. Some of these will already be familiar from school. You can assist your child to decode the ones they don't know by sounding out the letters.

As your child's confidence increases, you might like to pause at each word in bold and let your child try to sound it out for themselves. They can then practice the words again using the list at the back of the book.

After some time, your child may feel ready to tackle the whole story themselves. Maybe they can make up their own monster stories, too!

Sally Rippin is one of Australia's best-selling and most-beloved children's authors. She has written over 50 books for children and young adults, and her mantel holds numerous awards for her writing. Best known for her *Billie B. Brown*, *Hey Jack!* and *Polly and Buster* series, Sally loves to write stories with heart, as well as characters that resonate with children, parents, and teachers alike.

HOW TO DRAW BRUNO

① Using a pencil, start with 2 circles for eyes. Add 2 dots for eyeballs, a smaller circle for a nose, and a tuft of hair above the eyes.

② Now draw a happy smile and a large circle to make the mouth area. Connect the smile to the nose with a line, and add 2 pointy ears, one above each eye.

③ Draw in the top of the head and 2 hairy cheeks. Then add 2 box shapes for a vest.

④ Add some hairy arms and some zigzag lines for his ripped pants.

(5) Draw in the hands, some hairy legs, a belt, and a stripe coming down for his forehead.

(6) Time for the final details! Draw in some eyebrows, inside ear details, belly, and pointy teeth. Don't forget the spiky tail!

Chris Kennett has been drawing ever since he could hold a pencil (or so his mom says). But professionally, Chris has been creating quirky characters for just over 20 years. He's best known for drawing weird and wonderful creatures from the *Star Wars* universe, but he also loves drawing cute and cuddly monsters – and he hopes you do too!

WELCOME TO THE SCHOOL OF MONSTERS

Have you read **ALL** the School of Monsters stories?

START HERE

MARY HAS THE BEST PET

You shouldn't bring a pet to **school**. But Mary's pet is super **cool**!

HAIRY SAM LOVES BREAD AND JAM

Sam makes a mess when he eats **jam**. Can he fix it? Yes, he **can**!

PETE'S BIG FEET

Today it's Sports Day in the **sun**. But do you think that Pete can **run**?

BUG'S FIRST DAY

When Bug starts school he cannot **read**. But teacher has the help he **needs**!

JEM'S BIG IDEA

This is Jem. She likes to **play**, and thinks up fun new ways each **day**!

BRUNO WON'T DANCE

"Why won't Bruno dance?" says **Pat**. "There must be a fix for **that**!"

PIP LOVES TO COOK

Pip loves to cook and loves to **bake**. But will the monsters like her **cake**?

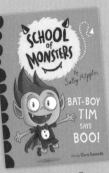

Now that you've learned to read along with Sally Rippin's School of Monsters, meet her other friends!

Hey Jack!

Billie B. Brown

Down-to-earth, real-life stories for real-life kids!

Billie B. Brown

Billie B. Brown is brave, brilliant and bold, and she always has a creative way to save the day!

Jack has a big heart and an even bigger imagination. He's Billie's best friend, and he'd love to be your friend, too!

Bruno Won't Dance

First American Edition 2023
Kane Miller, A Division of EDC Publishing

Text copyright © 2022 Sally Rippin
Illustration copyright © 2022 Chris Kennett
Series design copyright © 2022 Hardie Grant Children's Publishing
First published in 2022 by Hardie Grant Children's Publishing
Ground Floor, Building 1, 658 Church Street Richmond,
Victoria 3121, Australia.

For information contact:
Kane Miller, A Division of EDC Publishing
5402 S 122nd E Ave, Tulsa, OK 74146
www.kanemiller.com

Library of Congress Control Number: 2022952276

ISBN: 978-1-68464-748-4

Printed in China
10 9 8 7 6 5 4 3 2 1